#2

HOCKING GOBS OF PHLEGM

JIM LOPEZ

"The Last Dregs of Poverty"
Series

LSL
BOOKLETS

With a Queen of Heart embedded up a symbolic sleeve of the poorly written pages of thematic arts, uttered in the black hills of controversial words, echoing the need for a home and spiritual eyes, Mikey lost his way and walked the streets of Hollywood. He spat in the milk of growing children and pulled his pud in front of nursing mothers, who sat out front of Starbucks, sipping non-fat lattes.

Mikey had one ambition and one ambition only, he was writing a book titled, "The Adventures In The Unleashing of

Conventional Modes of Perception & Behavior," only he had no intention of ever putting pen to paper or fingers to keyboards. No, Mikey was the living pages of the title of his book, and it all started with a commercial and a bowl of cereal called LIFE that he was manipulated into peddling onto the rest of the world.

When Mikey was old enough to develop some awareness of himself he discovered that his life began with him being the cute and cuddly kid who hated everything and wouldn't try anything, yet he had to drink endless amounts of milk and shovel corn crisp day in and day out, while submental kids spurred him on, saying, "Let's get Mikey to try it, he hates everything," after which they cheered, "He likes it! He likes it!" But Mikey didn't hate everything he just hated everyone; nevertheless, he tried just about everything and now he had matured into a cynical masturbator and a phlegmatic.

As a child Mikey was forced to drink so much milk that he embodied a never ending factory of phlegm, and he hated milk, as well as LIFE cereal; neither of which were delicious nor nutritious. He was constantly hocking loogies. And when he felt the urge, which was more often than not, it was no big deal for him to whip out his wang and blast a wad of jizz on some unsuspecting passerby or on some mannequin displayed out in front of The GAP, J. Crew, Ann Taylor or any other business establishment. I mean, he just gooed his spooge anywhere and anytime.

Mikey refused to accept the line that was drawn between the public and private sphere. He urinated on dogs and in lady's purses (actually he pissed on whoever and whatever). He shit in mailboxes and on ATM machines, wiped his ass with cats, farted in the mouths of decrepit old people, knocked cripples down and out of his way, insulted and mocked the mentally challenged, slashed the tires of low-riding gang-bangers, punched business men in the face, ripped the underwear off of college students by giving them a rough wedgy, rebuked drug dealers and pimps while being a drug user and a whore monger himself. Mikey blew his nose on the pages of Walt Whitman's *Leaves of Grass*, he reviled Woodie Guthrie, Bob Dylan, The Beatles and anyone who could capture the spirit of humanity in song, he did all of this and terribly more. But what he did most was hock gobs of phlegm and chronically masturbated.

The first time I met Mikey I was having a bite to eat and a drink at the Pig and Whistle off of Hollywood Boulevard between Las Palmas and Highland. Mikey walked right up to my table, dropped his shorts, took a big shit directly on my mushroom burger and spit in my beer. And it served me right for eating in the fucking stink-hole of a place.

Now some tough guy might challenge me, asking, "Why didn't you stop the fucker or kick his ass?"

Well, I'd like to see someone not look stupidly surprised and shocked when some unsuspected freak flops a load on *your* food while *you're* reading the newspaper and enjoying a cigarette in between bites and drinks. There was no time. It was like, "What the fuck, there's a turd on my burger and a loogie in my beer." I mean, Mikey was the Pig and he went whistling down the street after he pulled some bald guy's wig off his head and wiped his ass with it after he shit on my mushroom burger. The sheer nerve and the audacious spirit of the guy was awe inspiring. He left a stench that lingered the distance between La Brea and Vine.

It made no difference what Mikey wiped his ass with as long as it remained wiped. That was his only concern, and he didn't lose any sleep trying to succumb to conventional or acceptable forms of material, like toilet paper. When it came to wiping his ass, Mikey was a strict utilitarian.

Mothers crossed busy boulevards and avenues to avoid walking on the same side of the street as Mikey. When the newspapers published that Mikey grabbed a swaddled infant out of her walker-crib and wiped his ass with the newly-budding baby Hollywood Boulevard went up in arms. Mikey argued in court that it was Hollywood herself that supported, even encouraged, his obscene behavior. According to the tabloids Little Mikey killed himself by ingesting too many Pop-Rocks while downing mass quantities of *RC-Cola*.

"I'm not even here. I don't exist. They killed me, Judge," he explained to the Honorable Magistrate. And as stupid and as asinine of an argument as it was, the fact of the matter remained, in a city like Hollywood, Mikey was, for all intents and purposes, dead: the little boy that America grew up with and ate breakfast with every morning was indeed dead. And the only way Mikey could affirm his existence was to use a runt's face to wipe his ass, because

Mikey had grown tired of people trying to convince him that he was no longer among the living.

Hollywood even produced a watered down version of the adult Mikey (played by Michael J. Fox), depicted as a wellman-nered slob, who stumbles into becoming a foster parent. Mikey contended that it was the press and concerned parents who initiated the rumor of his death.

"Someone with a lot of money wished to wipe out Pop-Rocks' profits, labeling them as dangerous when enhanced by *RC-Cola*, as this person wished to protect the pill-popping, speed-freak industry, which lived up in the Hills."

Mikey's trial was the headliner to a bill that included Isaac's fight with the City of Los Angeles. Issac was a black Jewish cabbalist, who could numerologically pinpoint who a person was and what a person would become. He also claimed to be one of the original GAP Band members, but was screwed out of his money and his job. He wasn't too pleased about being jilted. Isaac was also a regular at the Brass Monkey karaoke bar. I never saw the cat do karaoke. In fact, I suspect he avoided it, but he could be found shit-faced and acting up by 4:00 pm at the Monkey.

Isaac came into the courtroom, wearing torn-up pants and a dirty, white T-shirt. He was shoeless and had a potato sack overflowing with cotton slung over his back with a plastic ball-and-chain shackled to his ankle, shouting, "MAS-SER, why you always trying to keep the black man down?"

The press never got a whiff of Isaac's performance. But if you were there you were among God's true stars of Hollywood. The judge dismissed the case the moment Isaac came through the doors. He didn't even require him to pay the petty ten dollar charge for simply being granted the privilege to stand and be judged by an Honorable Magistrate.

Isaac had been booked, charged and released for ripping up a citation issued him for jay-walking and throwing the shredded ticket in the cop's face, shouting, "I'm a fifty-five-year-old man, if I don't know how to walk safely across the street you should lock me up, mother fucker! And I'd like to see you try. I'm a master numerologist. I'll fuck-up your celestial noodles!" (And Isaac could, but he never could figure out how the GAP Band screwed him out of his money.)

The Popo thought Isaac was threatening to kick him in the balls, so he arrested Isaac for terrorist's threats.

Mikey came into the courtroom wearing a six-hundred dollar pair of Romeo Gigli spectacles, a tailored white dress shirt and soiled boxer shorts, which depicted a stencil of Jake La Mada's busted-up face on the crouch. Mikey's extra-large balls could be seen periodically sagging just below his shorts, resembling a wad of chewed-up bubble gum. His feet were shod with florescent green flip-flops and his head was wrapped in a beach towel. He pleaded, "Not Guilty."

The judge refused to issue Mikey a trial date but called him into his chambers; after which, the case was dismissed when Mikey gave his word to never again wipe his ass with a child or any other featherlesss, two-legged creature. The mother of the child went bat-shit crazy, shouting that the judge was biased because Mikey had been a childhood star. It took every ounce of self-control that Mikey had to not grab the distraught mother and wipe his ass with her, but he gave his word, and whatever Mikey was he was no liar.

I followed Mikey out of the courthouse and onto the subway. He got off on Hollywood and Vine and then walked over to the abandoned World of Books store, where he and the one-legged Vietnam Vet, who daily polished the stars (one of which was Jimi Hendrix's) out front of the no longer existing World of Books book store. The two of them discussed how Mikey's case went that morning, and then they transitioned into a violent and bitter rant against the new developments of Hollywood Boulevard. They were about to head over to Grauman's Chinese Theater to defecate on John Wayne's and Bogart's hand and shoe prints but I talked Mikey into having a drink with me.

The Spot Lite was the hangout for convicted criminals, who happened to be transvestites, queers, and powerful prison queens, who could start full-blown prison wars. Mikey frequented the place, in fact, he would only have a drink with me if I agreed to buy him no more than two drinks at the Spot Lite.

I had never been in the Spot Lite, but I had walked by it numerous times throughout my life. On more than one occasion, I witnessed a burly transvestite pounding the shit out of some loud mouth, corn-fed redneck. I had also seen two, bearded transvestites bashing each other's heads on the pavement, into parked cars and against a steel garbage bin. These fellas were as tough as they were charming. I had also been catcalled a few times by a transvestite smoking outside the Spot Lite, and I was always able to deflect the gesture with a little flirtation of my own or pleasantly ignore it, but I sure as hell wasn't indifferent; rather, I was slightly terrified by the place. Once, I'd even seen a prison bus stop in front of the Spot Lite and drop off a number of transvestites and queers.

The place was dark and damp. The vinyl barstools were cracked and crusty. The walls were black and sticky. Jimmy Boyd's *Jelly On My Head* was playing at a pleasant volume through the jukebox.

Mikey ordered a glass of Lagavulin Scotch from his private stash, which the Spot Lite kept for him behind the bar and only charged him five dollars a glass. He kept a bottle there attempting to acquiesce to his doctor's orders, who demanded that he stop drinking. Once a month he would buy a bottle of the Scotch, walk over to the Spot Lite and hand it to the bartender, who would open it for him, pour him a glass, charge him the additional five dollars and then place the rest of the bottle on the top shelf behind the Jim Beam. Mikey had one glass of Lagavulin every four days but today he wanted two. I ordered the only top shelf Bourbon the Spot Lite offered, Jim Beam.

"So, what the fuck do you want?" Mikey asked me.

"I'm not quite sure," I answered stupidly. "Last month, at the Pig and Whistle, you shit on my mushroom burger and spit in my beer."

"Yeah, so what, you shouldn't have been eating at the fucking cunt-hole of a place. You're not a sensitive twat are you? I'd wipe my ass with you right here and now if I hadn't given my word to the judge this morning. Piss me off and I'll have one of these bitchy skag-draggers turn you into a sailor's cup of tea as they corn-hole your pooper. Hey, Lonnie, come over here. I want to introduce you to someone."

"Fuck you, Mikey, can't you see I'm busy," Lonnie shouted as the she-male was bent over the pool table, attempting a three-ball-combo in the side pocket, with his sundress hiked up to his waist, and his sweaty ass hairs dangling out of his ruffled panties, which were stretched tight around his fat ass.

The jukebox switched to John Rox's *I Want A Hippopotamus for Christmas,* sung by the child star, Gayla Peevey, who became a whisker on the Easter Bunnies chin, hiding eggs from children, and never growing larger than *Thumbelina*'s toe.

The Spot Lite was getting moist and ornery.

"No, you're quite right. I thought the same thing myself: the burger stunk, the beer was shit and it was all well over-priced," I nervously but whole heartedly agreed.

"Like a fucking Hollywood film or Bushwhack My Bottom's bailout."

After a long silence Mikey asked, "So you don't know why you asked me for a drink?"

"Well, I guess I'd like to know what sort of women find you a attractive, I mean..."

"Take a look around this place. It's

fair to say that the omens have fore-shadowed bad fucks for Little Mikey. There ain't no Haley's Comet blazing a path in my sky," Mikey answered. Then he wrung his drink and asked me to order him another one.

A buffed-out Austrian transvestite, who didn't make the cut for the Viennese Boys Choir, answered a call from Warner Brothers, but found himself in an entirely different line of work than he expected, was going around the bar showing off his scrog scrapbook, which depicted the she-male getting screwed by politicians and Hollywood producers. He was singing and whistling, "I only cost a nickel and if that's too much for you, take me for a penny and I'll thank you kindly."

"I'm sick of the Hollywood prattle, where permeability saturates morality and is hypocritically regarded over aggressive penetration," Mikey muttered irritably, as his eyes turned gargoyle green. He spit a loogie over the bar and onto the cash register. Miley was visibly growing more and more agitated, quoting Mark Twain, *A monotonous career of violence and bloodshed*, then he pounded his second drink.

I didn't understand what he was getting at.

All of a sudden Mikey jumped on top of the bar, ripped the towel off his head, tugged down his Jake La Mada boxer shorts and flopped a turd right on the bar.

"God-damn-it, Mikey, not again!" Ernie, the bartender rebuked him.

"My freedom demands it this time, Ernie, so fuck-off!" Mikey shouted, flipping everyone the bird (like Flipper the Dolphin), bulging his eyes and smacking his butt cheeks, as he pissed in the bar-well. Then he dove on a man, who strangely resembled a famous Hollywood Producer I had recognized at Mikey's courtroom hearing. The Hollywood Producer looked more amorous than frightened. Mikey unashamedly shit-fucked the man, who unashamedly offered up his rump for all to take more than a gander; and there was indeed "quite" a number of "quite" large and greasy tranies pounding their meat across his face.

The tapestry devil was doing a pirouette, fanning flagrant fellatios. Then I saw something that baffled me all together: the judge, who presided over Mikey's case, had slipped into the Spot Lite undetected and was now jacking-off in a dark corner wearing a Mickey Mouse hat.

I held my ass and snuck out of this

bestial ballroom, which was reminiscent of a Greek Philosopher's after-party, as the jukebox dropped another Jimmy Boyd 45: *There's A Little Train Chuggin' In My Heart.*

www.ingramcontent.com/pod-product-compliance
Lightning Source LLC
Chambersburg PA
CBHW020613130626
46552CB00007B/3183